DEDICATED TO LOUIS & OTIS

LITTLE PENGUIN WAS EXTREMELY EXCITED AS IT WAS THE NIGHT BEFORE HIS BIRTHDAY.

"IT WILL BE HARD TO SLEEP TONIGHT, MOTHER PENGUIN. I REALLY CANNOT WAIT UNTIL I HAVE MY PARTY TOMORROW – AND MY BIRTHDAY CAKE!"

"I KNOW, LITTLE PENGUIN. I AM VERY EXCITED TOO. I HAVE GOT YOU PLENTY OF MILK AS A BIRTHDAY TREAT," SAID MOTHER PENGUIN.

BROTHER PENGUIN WAS IN HIS BEDROOM AND PUTTING THE FINISHING TOUCHES TO HIS PRESENT FOR LITTLE PENGUIN.

THIS YEAR HE HAD MADE HIM A REALLY COOL FOOTBALL GOAL. BROTHER PENGUIN WOULD STRUGGLE AT TIMES WITH MAKING THINGS LIKE THIS.

LUCKILY MOTHER PENGUIN WAS THERE TO HELP.

"MOTHER PENGUIN, DO YOU THINK THE NET IS STRONG ENOUGH? I AM REALLY WORRIED THAT IF LITTLE PENGUIN HITS THE BALL TOO HARD IT MAY GO THROUGH," ASKED BROTHER PENGUIN.

"DO NOT WORRY, BROTHER PENGUIN. I HAVE SUPERGLUED THE NET EXTRA TIGHT," SAID MOTHER PENGUIN.

FATHER PENGUIN WAS MAKING LITTLE PENGUIN'S FAVOURITE SANDWICHES FOR THE PARTY.

"I THINK I MAY NEED MORE CHEESE," SAID FATHER PENGUIN.

LITTLE PENGUIN LOVED CHEESE SANDWICHES.

MOTHER, BROTHER AND LITTLE PENGUIN WERE ALL IN THE LIVING ROOM PUTTING UP DECORATIONS FOR THE PARTY.

"I CANNOT WAIT TO SEE GRANDAD PENGUIN AND NANNY PENGUIN TOMORROW," SAID LITTLE PENGUIN. "I REALLY HOPE NANNY PENGUIN MAKES HER SPECIAL CHOCOLATE CAKE."

LITTLE PENGUIN WAS GETTING READY FOR BED. HE WAS WONDERING IF HE WOULD EVER GET TO SLEEP AS HE WAS SO EXCITED ABOUT THE BIG PARTY FOR HIS BIRTHDAY THE NEXT DAY.

"I CAN'T WAIT TO SEE MY FAMILY AND PLAY GAMES ON MY BIRTHDAY," LITTLE PENGUIN SAID TO HIS BROTHER.

"ME TOO," SAID BROTHER PENGUIN. "I HOPE GRANDAD BRINGS HIS FOOTBALL BOOTS WITH HIM."

"WHY IS THAT?" ASKED LITTLE PENGUIN.

BROTHER PENGUIN WENT VERY SHY AND HIS CHEEKS WENT VERY RED.

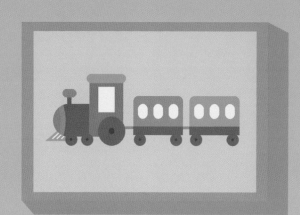

IT WAS THE MORNING OF LITTLE PENGUIN'S BIRTHDAY AND EVERYONE IN THE HOUSE WAS VERY EXCITED. MOTHER PENGUIN HAD DECORATED EVERY ROOM IN THE HOUSE FOR LITTLE'S BIG DAY.

"HAPPY BIRTHDAY!" MOTHER, FATHER AND BROTHER PENGUIN CHEERED.

LITTLE PENGUIN WAS SO HAPPY AND WAS LOOKING FORWARD TO SEEING HIS FAMILY AND OPENING HIS PRESENTS.

LITTLE PENGUIN HAD RECEIVED SOME WONDERFUL GIFTS FROM HIS FAMILY AND WAS SO HAPPY WITH HIS NEW FOOTBALL GOAL FROM HIS BROTHER.

"THIS IS THE BEST PRESENT EVER!" LITTLE PENGUIN SAID. "THANK YOU VERY MUCH BROTHER PENGUIN. I NOW KNOW WHY YOU WANTED GRANDAD PENGUIN TO BRING HIS FOOTBALL BOOTS WITH HIM."

THE DOORBELL RANG. IT WAS GRANDAD AND NANNY PENGUIN.

"HAPPY BIRTHDAY LITTLE PENGUIN!" THEY BOTH SAID.

"I HAVE BROUGHT YOUR FAVOURITE CHOCOLATE CAKE," SAID
NANNY PENGUIN.

"THIS IS ALREADY THE BEST BIRTHDAY EVER!" SHOUTED LITTLE PENGUIN. "GRANDAD, DID YOU BRING YOUR FOOTBALL BOOTS?"

"I SURE DID!" SAID GRANDAD PENGUIN.

LITTLE AND BROTHER PENGUIN WERE SO EXCITED TO PLAY FOOTBALL WITH GRANDAD PENGUIN AND LITTLE'S BRAND NEW GOAL.

GRANDAD, BROTHER AND LITTLE PENGUIN ALL WENT TO THE GARDEN TO PLAY FOOTBALL.

THEY WERE OUT THERE FOR HOURS! THIS MADE LITTLE PENGUIN'S DAY – IT WAS A BIRTHDAY HE WOULD NEVER FORGET!

Printed in Great Britain
by Amazon